Other Black Bear Sled Dog Adventures....

Black Bear Goes to Washington

Black Bear Goes to San Francisco

Black Bear Saves Christmas

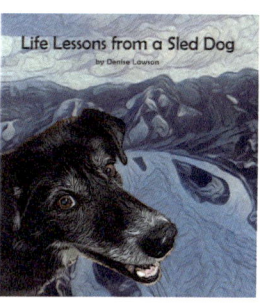
Life Lessons from a Sled Dog

What do sled dogs do when they can no longer pull a sled? Follow Black Bear on her journeys of discovery in the Black Bear Sled Dog book series. This book series helps support retired Alaskan sled dogs.

Visit **www.blackbearsleddog.com** for interactive games and more information about Black Bear.

The Midwest Book Review highly recommends the Black Bear book series for young readers.

"Entertaining, thoroughly 'kid friendly' in commentary and presentation, thoughtful and thought-provoking, 'Life Lessons from a Sled Dog' is especially and unreservedly recommended for family, daycare center, preschool, elementary school, and community library picture book collections."

Midwest Book Review: Children's Bookwatch

Dedicated to retired sled dogs everywhere.

Copyright © 2020 by Denise Lawson
All rights reserved. No part of this book may be reproduced in any form or by any electronic or mechanical means, including information storage and retrieval systems, without permission in writing from the publisher, except by reviewers, who may quote brief passages in a review.

First Edition

ISBN 978-1-7355048-0-3

Library of Congress Control Number: 2020943120
Printed in the United States of America

Published by Brown & Lowe Books
Springfield, VA
www.brownlowebooks.com

Run Like a Sled Dog
Another Black Bear Sled Dog Adventure

Written and Illustrated by
Denise Lawson

This book was inspired by a visit to The PrAiry Farm where Black Bear shared her sled dog tales with a very special sheep.

Thanks Gordon for all you do to help bring these sled dog dreams to life. – D.A.L.

While some folks are busy counting sheep,
Others have sled dog dreams in their sleep!

I arrived at the farm on a very hot day,
The sheep in the fields were too tired to play.

The farmer had sled dog chores to be done,
But oh, too much work to do for just one.

How can I pull this heavy load over there?
Without any help, it seems quite unfair.

I don't see any sled dogs out in the yard.
What other animals can pull very hard?

An extra harness is needed. I do have a spare.
Is anyone willing to help? I'm willing to share!

If maybe, just maybe, the harness will fit,
We can get the job done, lickety-split!

I think Hoot, the Alpaca, looks very strong,
But the harness won't fit him. His neck is too long.

What about that rooster I see strutting around?
He said, "Sorry, my job is to make a loud sound!"

Kazoo, I know is a very strong horse,
But his belly is too large for my harness, of course.

Buzz, buzz, buzz...there goes a busy bee!
He's definitely too small to pull a load with me.

What about Camilla, the very strong cow?
She's busy grazing in the fields right now.

Along came a sheep who was just the right size,
The answer was standing in front of my eyes!

Sled sheep or sheep dog? What should it be,
If a sheep pulls a sled before afternoon tea?

All harnessed up, Tink had a new dream,
To mush in Alaska on a real sled dog team.

Whenever you think something cannot be done,
Just be like a sled dog, and get out and run!